She REALIZED THAT She COULD TOO

by
Jasmine Alagoz
and Kian Alagoz

To order additional copies of this book, contact:
Xlibris
844-714-8691
www.Xlibris.com
Orders@Xlibris.com

ISBN:	Softcover	978-1-6698-4478-5
	EBook	978-1-6698-4479-2

Print information available on the last page

Rev. date: 10/05/2022

She
REALIZED
THAT She
COULD
TOO

Sitting at her desk, eagerly waiting for her teacher to hand her back her test,

She couldn't help but notice her classmates' faces, gleaming with joy after seeing their score.

Her teacher came to her side and handed her the test.

She was surprised;

Seeing all the bright red marks all over her paper was concerning.

She was confused;

Her classmates all seemed to do well on their test, not a red mark in sight.

But she was unhappy.

She studied, and she felt prepared.

But it wasn't enough

She felt helpless.
If she couldn't do it,
Then she wasn't good enough.

To tell you a little bit more about Lily,

She had a dream, a big one.

She wanted to be a doctor, a surgeon to be exact.

Seeing how doctors can save lives for a living inspired her;

She wanted to save lives too.

There was just one problem:

She couldn't get the grades that she wanted.

She was never the smartest girl in the class.

She was never the girl that could understand what she was learning

She felt helpless.
If she couldn't do it,
Then she wasn't good enough.

Lily's best friend was her mother.

She felt like she could tell her anything.

One day, she asked her mother,

"Mom, what should I do? I can't seem to do as good as my classmates?"

Her mother looked at her lovingly and said, "As long as you are trying your best, you have done enough."

Lily carried her mother's advice.
She continued to try her best,
Even if the results weren't as good as she expected.

Then Lily went off to college.

There, she had several more failures.

Even though she tried her best,

She began to question herself and her dreams.

She felt helpless.
If she couldn't do it,
Then she wasn't good enough.

Lily still wanted to fulfill her childhood dream of becoming a doctor,

But she did not think that she would be accepted

Because her classmates performed better than her.

She felt helpless.
If she couldn't do it,
Then she wasn't good enough.

But suddenly, her mother's words came into her mind:

"As long as you are trying your best, you have done enough."

She decided to take a chance.

She wanted to prove to herself that she could do it.

There she was, sitting on her computer,
Waiting to get her admission decision,
But this time things were different.

She opened her e-mail; to her surprise,
She was accepted.
She now has the opportunity to save lives.

In medical school, she was surrounded by people who would do better than her,

But Lily did not forget the valuable lesson she had learned—

To always try her best;

That would be enough.

While she was never the smartest girl in the class,

She studied and continued to work hard to achieve her dream.

Finally, all her hard work paid off.

She felt optimistic.

If she put in the hard work,

Then she was good enough.

Now you may wonder what happened to Lily.

She is now working in a hospital, performing life-changing surgeries on cancer patients.

She now can save lives,
All because of her mother's words:

"As long as you are trying your best, you have done enough."

She has done enough.

Lily learned the valuable lesson that success comes from hard work.

It isn't about how well you do compared to others;

It's about trying your best and never giving up.

Once she took a chance and believed in herself,

She realized she could too.

Printed in the United States
by Baker & Taylor Publisher Services